THE GHOSTS OF BATWING CASTLE

Terry Deary

Illustrated by Shoo Rayner

Galaxy

CHIVERS PRESS
BATH

First published in 1988
by
A & C Black Publishers Ltd
This Large Print edition published by
BBC Audiobooks Ltd.
by arrangement with
A & C Black Publishers Ltd
2003

ISBN 0 7540 7869 8

British Library Cataloguing in Publication Data

Deary, Terry
   The ghosts of Batwing Castle.—Large print ed.
   1. Haunted castles—Juvenile fiction 2. Ghost stories
   3. Children's stories 4. Large type books
   I. Title II. Rayner, Shoo
   823. 9'14[J]
ISBN 0-7540-7869-8

Printed and bound in Great Britain by
Antony Rowe Ltd., Chippenham, Wiltshire

CHAPTER ONE

THE ROAD TO BATWING CASTLE

The Castle sat on the hill like an ugly grey toad in the moonlight.

A narrow road twisted through a tangle of hedges. There wasn't a sound in the frost-bright night till the grumbling roar of a speeding car cracked the cold air.

A girl in patched and tattered jeans stopped on the road and listened. She shivered silently. The car was coming her way and she knew there was nowhere to hide.

She shrank into the hedge till the gorse-spines snatched at her long, black hair and she peered back down the silver ribbon of road.

No golden glow of headlights; only the gargling sound of an engine growing steadily louder. Suddenly she saw it! A purple shadow on the diamond-grey road—a small sports-car rushing blind and lightless up the hill towards her.

The girl screamed, and at that moment the driver saw her white and frightened face and he swerved. The car bounced off the wall of hedge with the tearing screech of a thousand thorns and slithered to a stop.

The driver turned and glared with eyes that were just shadowy slits in a podgy, freckled face. 'Watch where you're walking, shorty!' he said.

'You had no lights on!' the girl protested.

'Neither had you!' the driver snapped back. His voice was as thin as a penny-whistle and it made the girl peer at him.

'You're not old enough to drive a car,' she gasped.

'And you're not old enough to be out alone at this time of night,' the boy argued.

'You were going too fast,' she said.

'You were going too slow,' he snapped back. 'And what are you doing on this road anyway?'

The girl threw back her head defiantly. 'I'm going to Batwing Castle to find the treasure—they say it only appears once every ten years or so when the full moon falls on . . .'

'I know, I know!' the boy cut in crossly. 'And it's guarded by a groaning ghost and a vicious vampire,' the podgy boy went on with a sneer on his face. Suddenly he stuck his face forward. 'Want a lift, skinny?'

'Well . . . I . . .'

'Hah! Listen! I'm Wilkin T Wilkins—the richest boy in Toominster . . .' he said.

'And I'm Mary Stone—my friends call me Molly—I'm probably the poorest girl in Toominster,' she put in quickly.

But the boy didn't seem to be listening.

'Most girls would be glad of a lift in a car driven by Wilkin T Wilkins—my friends call me "Sir".'

'Oh, I *would* like a lift, thank you, but are you sure you're old enough to drive?'

'Course I'm not . . . but I *am* quite safe. Father taught me on our private airfield and he even loaned me one of his cars.' He frowned and rubbed a silvery bramble-scar that had spoiled the blood-red paint. 'Get in!' he ordered.

Molly Stone stepped into the car and trembled as the boy started the powerful motor.

'I hope I won't be taking you out of your way,' she said politely.

'Of course not,' Wilkin T Wilkins whined. 'I'm going to the castle too.'

'To find the treasure?' Molly asked as the car surged forward.

'To find the treasure,' the boy giggled. The wind began to gush through the car windows as it rushed along the road.

'But you don't need the money,' Molly shouted so she could be heard over the roaring of air and engine. 'You seem rich enough already.'

'I don't *need* it,' Wilkin T cackled, 'but I still *want* it! As well as being the richest boy in Toominster I am also the *greediest!*'

And the wind whipped his whistling laughter into the star-speckled night.

4

CHAPTER TWO

FRIDAY THE THIRTEENTH

Wilkin T Wilkins had a mouth like a frog—a rather ugly frog at that. Thin-lipped and always curved in a smug smile as if to tell the world how wonderful it was to be Wilkin T Wilkins.

'I'm running away from home,' he giggled. 'I'll find the treasure and then I needn't ever go home again.'

'Don't you like your home, then?' Molly asked, and she suddenly felt sorry for the boastful boy.

'No,' he hissed. 'Does anyone? Do you?'

'Well ... I ...'

'My father is a pig,' Wilkin T said sourly.

'You mean he eats a lot?' Molly asked.

The boy gave her a hard and nasty stare. 'No, stupid. Your brain must be as thin as your body. I mean he's rotten to me.'

'But he loaned you his car,' she reminded him.

Wilkin T gripped the steering wheel hard and peered at the twisting road. 'He didn't exactly *lend* it to me . . . I just sort of borrowed it.'

'Stole it!' Molly said.

The fat boy's froggy face turned fierce. 'It isn't stealing if you take something from your own parents.'

Molly was just about to argue when he swung the steering-wheel and the car lurched across the road. The tyres wailed and smoked like a cat with its tail on fire. 'What was that?' Molly gasped.

'Hedgehog!'

'Did you miss it?' the girl asked, biting her knuckle.

'Yes,' Wilkin T snarled.

'Oh, well done,' she sighed and patted his arm.

'What do you mean, "well done"? I was swerving to *hit* the spikey little rat!'

Molly took her hand from the boy's arm and huddled deep into the soft, leather seat. 'You're not a very pleasant boy,' she said.

'And you're not a very *un*pleasant girl,' the driver cackled as he swerved and swayed his way to the top of the twisting road. Molly sighed and pushed a whipping wisp of hair from her face.

'If I find the treasure I'll give it to my mum and dad to buy a new house,' she said.

'Why?' Wilkin T asked suddenly.

'Why? . . . because it would make them happy,' the girl explained.

'Yeuch,' Wilkin T croaked. 'You're a real little goody-goody, aren't you? I hate goody-goodies.' Before Molly could answer he went on, 'Anyway, you won't *get* the gold, Miss Goody-guts. I will!'

'Won't you share it?' she asked.

'Nope!' the boy said and his mouth shut like a fly-trap plant.

'If *I* found it I'd share it with you,' Molly offered.

'You wouldn't,' Wilkin T sneered. 'If *you* found it first I'd take it *from* you. Heh!'

'In that case I think it would be

7

better if you dropped me off here,' the girl said firmly.

'O.K.,' Wilkin T replied. 'If that's what you want, cheerio!' But the car raced on.

After a minute Molly asked, 'Why aren't you stopping so that I can get out?'

'Why aren't you *jumping* if you want to get out?' Wilkin T answered. 'We're nearly there anyway.'

Sure enough, the track began to widen into a broad avenue bordered by tall, sad trees. The castle stood at the end of the tunnel of trees. It seemed to shimmer and glow in its greyness like a great elephant-flavoured jelly. Wilkin T switched off the car engine and rolled to a halt in front of the huge gates. The sudden silence hurt Molly's ears. Even Wilkin T felt he had to whisper.

'This is it! Batwing Castle. And the treasure can only be found once every ten years or so, when the full moon falls on Friday the thirteenth,' he said softly. 'That's tonight.'

'Tonight,' Molly murmured.

'Tonight!' A creaking voice came from behind Molly's back and her blood ran cold.

9

CHAPTER THREE

BATWING CASTLE CARETAKER

'Can I help you?' the voice went on. Molly turned round slowly and found herself looking into the eye of an old man dressed a bit like a bus conductor in a limp blue uniform. His right eye looked large as a golf-ball and glinted in the light of the rising moon. His left eye was the same size as Molly's, but she hardly noticed it.

'I . . . er . . . I . . . er . . .' she stammered.

Wilkin T Wilkins stepped forward and pushed Molly firmly aside. 'Good evening, my man,' he said, stretching out a hand. Instead of shaking it the old man turned a torch on the boy's face. For the first time Molly was able to see that the fat face was pink as a piglet and covered in freckles. 'My name is Wilkin T Wilkins . . . you may have heard of me . . .'

'Can't say that I have,' the old man said scratching the rough white stubble on his chin. 'And what's your name, young lady?' he asked.

'Mary . . . Mary Stone,' she said quietly.

The odd eye was fearsome but the old face around it seemed kindly enough.

'Ah, *Mary*, is it? Tell me, girl, do they ever call you *Molly*?' he asked, and his golf-ball eye rolled like a bobbing beach-ball.

'Oh, yes. At home they always call me Molly,' she said.

The old man nodded his head sharply. 'The ghost will be interested to hear that.'

'Hah! Ghost! Hah!' Wilkin T exploded. 'Tosh and ten-ton tiddlers!

There are no such things as ghosts. That's just a story put about to scare people away from the treasure! Why, I bet you're after the treasure yourself, you smelly little man,' the boy went on.

'I don't want the treasure! The vampire wouldn't let me past to get near it!' the old man choked and fear flashed through his eye.

'Hah! Vampires now! No such things as vampires! Another one of your stories,' Wilkin T crowed. 'If you're not after the treasure yourself then what are you doing here, eh? Answer that! Answer that! Answer that! Can't, can you? Eh? Eh? Eh?' Wilkin T said, prodding the old man's chest with his fat little finger.

The old man sighed. 'I'm here because it's my job to be here. I'm the caretaker of Batwing Castle. Mr Toon's the name . . . the young people call me Pop—it's their idea of a joke. *Pop Toon*. Get it?'

'You wouldn't get in my top twenty, Pop Toon,' Wilkin T sneered. 'Not unless you had a bath first!' he went on rudely.

The old man hardly seemed to notice Wilkin's words as he fumbled in his pocket. After a few moments he pulled out a small book. 'Want to buy a guidebook?' he asked, suddenly thrusting the book under Wilkin's button nose. 'Has a map of the castle inside!'

'How much is it?' Wilkin asked.

'How much can you afford?' he asked.

'A million pounds!' Wilkin boasted.

'Then a million pounds it is,' Mr Toon said with a gap-toothed grin.

'Will you take a cheque?' the boy asked.

'No,' the old man answered.

'Then I won't have one,' Wilkin

sniffed. 'You can keep your tatty little guidebook.'

Pop Toon shrugged and said, 'You'll never find the treasure without one.'

Molly stepped forward. 'I have ten pence; that's all I can afford. Will you sell *me* one?' she asked.

The old caretaker sighed. 'I would, but it would be better if you didn't go after the treasure, young lady.' His voice dropped to a croak. 'There's danger for whoever seeks it.'

Molly sank back until she was sitting on the bumper bar of the red sports car. She ran a hand through her hair and spoke quietly. 'I *have* to find the treasure. You see, my parents couldn't find any work in Toominster and we became very poor. Then Dad found a job—the trouble is it's a hundred miles away. We never see him now, and we miss him ever so much . . . especially Mum. If I could only find the treasure we'd be able to get our dad back.'

'We'll have to see what we can do,' the caretaker said softly, and he pushed the guidebook into her pocket.

CHAPTER FOUR

INTO THE CASTLE

The castle loomed huge in the moon's gloomy light. Wilkin T Wilkins boldly led the way to the wooden drawbridge. The caretaker and Molly Stone followed more slowly.

'Ghosts!' jeered the boy. 'I'll believe in ghosts when you show me one,' he said.

'In that case, you'd better start believing because you're looking at one,' old Pop Toon said with a chuckle.

Wilkin T stopped suddenly. 'Ghost? What ghost? I can't see any ghost!'

'I can't either, Mr Toon,' Molly admitted.

The caretaker turned to her. 'Have you ever seen Batwing Castle before tonight?' he asked and his large eye gleamed gleefully.

'Why, yes,' Molly said. 'We used to come for picnics in the ruins. And the school once took us to visit the waxworks in the dungeons . . . *The Chamber of Terrors* they called it.'

'Hah! Just goes to show how much you know, stupid,' Wilkin T scoffed. 'This castle isn't a ruin at all. In fact it looks as good as new.'

'Exactly!' the caretaker said excitedly. 'The real castle is a ruin—but when the full moon falls on Friday the thirteenth then the ghost of the old castle appears.'

'You mean the castle itself is a ghost?' Molly asked.

Mr Toon nodded till his navy cap almost fell off his head. 'It is. Most of this will vanish at sunrise.'

'And is the treasure ghostly as well?' Molly asked. 'I mean, will *it* vanish at sunrise too?'

'Oh, no. The treasure is real enough. It still lies where it was hidden, six hundred years ago, by the fourth Duchess of Batwing,' Mr Toon explained. 'The trouble is it can only be found by following the old walls and doors and stairs—and you can only see them when the ghostly Batwing Castle appears.'

'Hah!' Wilkin T cried. 'What a story! If you think I'm going to believe that pathetic piffle then you're a looney, Tooney!' He stepped forward on to the drawbridge. He jumped on it till the booming of his fat feet echoed off the cold walls. 'See! Solid as your head, old man.'

The caretaker nodded. 'The water in that moat seems real as well,' he said, pointing his torch at the mirror-smooth water. 'But you could drink a bucketful and still be thirsty.'

'I don't drink water,' Wilkin said grandly. 'Only wine.' And with that he strutted across the drawbridge into the shadowy arch of the castle gateway.

'He's going to come to a very nasty end, that young man,' the caretaker murmured to Molly.

'He's very brave,' she said.

'Humph. Brave isn't as good as clever. Sometimes it pays to be scared. If you're scared then you're careful—if you're brave then you can get careless. And Batwing Castle is so dangerous that you can't afford to get careless for even a moment. If the vampires don't get you then the treasure-trap will.'

'Treasure-trap,' Molly said with a shudder. 'What's that?'

'You'll see,' the old man promised. 'You'll see.'

He hurried across the phantom drawbridge and came alongside Wilkin T Wilkins who stood at the gateway and stared into the castle courtyard. When Molly reached his side she discovered the sight that had stopped him.

The castle was glowing in the amber-gold light of a hundred flaming torches. Silky smoke curled up into the midnight air to mask the moon. The hiss and the sputter of the fires scratched through the silence of the scene. Suddenly the dead, dreary castle seemed alive as if the stones themselves were holding their breath and waiting for the human visitors to make some move.

'It's beautiful,' Molly breathed.

'Saves on the electricity bill,' Wilkin T joked, but his voice had a slight tremble to it.

'Where do we go now, Mr Toon?' the girl asked.

'Follow the guidebook. That's what you need to do,' the old man said, tapping the copy in the girl's pocket.

'Aren't you coming with us?' she asked.

He shook his head. 'This is where I leave you, child.' He stared at her and his large eye looked sadly worried as it caught the flickering light of the torches. 'Take care. And remember— be afraid! Better to be dead frightened than to be dead-dead.'

As he vanished through a dark doorway she cried, 'But who'll help us?'

'Don't worry, I will,' called the mournful voice of the Batwing Castle ghost.

CHAPTER FIVE

CYRIL THE GHOST

Wilkin T Wilkins sighed. He looked up at the stone stairway that led to the castle walls. A thin, pitiful figure of a boy sat there. His hair was wild as a west wind and the bony face beneath was thinner than an east wind. 'Don't tell me, you're the ghost of Batwing Castle.'

The thin boy seemed to brighten. 'Oh, so you've heard of me then?'

Wilkin T's slit eyes narrowed still further. 'I don't believe in ghosts.'

'Oh, I'm sorry,' the ghost said, looking hurt.

'So come down from those stairs at once, I need some help to find the treasure,' the fat boy ordered.

'Yes, sir!' the ghost replied. There was a faint popping sound and the figure of the skinny boy disappeared. An instant later it appeared in front of Wilkin T Wilkins. Molly gasped and

even Wilkin looked a little startled. 'My name is Cyril and I'm at your service, sir.'

Wilkin T blinked. 'How did you do that vanishing trick?' he snapped.

'Oh, all ghosts can do that,' Cyril said. 'It's about the only exciting thing a ghost can do, you know. That and walking through walls. But after a while even that gets boring. You know, it's terribly, terribly boring being a ghost. And it's so *cold*. You wouldn't believe how cold it is!'

Wilkin T sighed again. 'You are not a ghost.'

'No, sir, if you say so sir,' the ghost said miserably.

'Then how did he vanish from the stairs?' Molly asked.

'Just a trick,' Wilkin T explained grandly. 'An illusion. Stage magic—like when a magician makes a rabbit appear in a hat.'

'Oh, I can't do that, sir!' Cyril said quickly.

'Then you're not a very good magician,' Wilkin T sneered.

'No, sir,' Cyril answered, 'I'm not. I'm not even a very good ghost. I've never scared anyone in five hundred years.'

'You scared me!' Molly put in.

Suddenly the ghost-pale face cracked into a huge grin. 'Did I?' Cyril said eagerly. 'Did I really? Oh, thanks for saying so, miss. Thank you!'

'You are not a ghost and you have not been here for five hundred years,' Wilkin T said sternly.

The ghostly grin faded. 'No, sir . . . sorry, sir . . . I forgot, sir!' the thin boy muttered.

'I believe you,' Molly said gently and

24

the ghost smiled shyly at her.

'Hah!' Wilkin T exploded. 'Stay and talk to this soap-faced scarecrow if you want, but I'm off to do some exploring.' And the fat boy began to wander round the castle courtyard peering into windows and rattling door handles.

Molly sat on the bottom step of the stairway and hugged her thin anorak around her knees. 'It must be very lonely being a ghost,' she said.

'Oh, it is, miss, it is!' Cyril said and he drifted down to settle beside her. 'Even the vampire of Batwing Castle won't bother with me because I have no blood to suck . . .'

'There's really a vampire here, then?' Molly asked with a shudder. 'I hope it won't bother with me either.'

'I'll try to protect you,' Cyril promised. 'I'll try.'

'Don't you ever have any other visitors?' the girl asked.

'Only human ones. The brave ones who want to spend a night in a haunted castle. I soon drive them away though,' the ghost sighed.

Molly turned to him, puzzled. 'I

thought you said that you never scared anyone.'

Cyril nodded. 'That's right. I couldn't scare a mouse to death, let alone a ghost-hunter. No, you see, I *bore* them to death!' The ghost's pale face looked as long as a wet weekend in winter.

'You don't bore me,' Molly said.

'Ah, but you're not a ghost-hunter looking for excitement, are you? What have I got to offer? I mean, the Tower of London has old Anne Boleyn doing clever tricks like tucking her head underneath her arm. All I can do is wander round moaning and groaning. You have to admit, that's about as exciting as being bitten by a flea.'

'Couldn't you tuck your head underneath your arm?' Molly suggested.

'Tried it once, miss,' Cyril moaned. 'I dropped it in the moat by accident. Took me a hundred and twelve years to find it. It's hard looking for something when you haven't got a head, miss.'

Molly smiled. 'You don't have to call me *miss*—my name is Molly.' As she said this the ghost jumped like a frightened ferret.

'Molly!' he moaned. 'I always knew you'd come back for me. Darling Molly!'

CHAPTER SIX

CYRIL'S SAD STORY

'Five hundred years I've waited for you, Molly,' the ghost of Batwing Castle cried, and he fluttered like a torch-flame in the breeze.

'Not for me, Cyril, not for me!' Molly Stone cried quickly. 'It must have been another Molly you knew.'

Cyril drifted back on to the step and looked carefully into the girl's face. At last he said quietly, 'No, perhaps not.'

Then he brightened. 'But it is a sign, I'm sure. A good sign. You arriving tonight of all nights. Perhaps by sunrise I'll be free at last.'

'Free?' Molly asked.

The ghost nodded. 'Free of the treasure-trap.'

'What is this treasure-trap? Mr Toon the caretaker spoke of it but he didn't tell me what it was. What *is* it? How did you get into the trap?' Molly said.

'It's a long story,' the ghost moaned.

28

'I'll probably bore you away if I try to tell it.'

Molly shook her head. 'I'm a good listener,' she promised. 'Go on. Tell me all about it—about you . . . and Molly . . . and the treasure-trap.'

Cyril sighed and settled himself again.

'I may be a boring old ghost,' he said, 'but when I was alive I wasn't boring, I can tell you.'

'I'm sure you weren't,' Molly said eagerly.

'Oh, no. I was the life and soul of the castle kitchen,' Cyril went on.

'You worked there, did you?' Molly asked.

'No. My job was stable-lad. But all the servants used to gather in the kitchens after a day's work, to have the evening meal together. They'd all be sitting there at the big oak table and I'd come in with my merry quips and jolly jokes. They loved me. "Oh, no!" they'd cry as I walked in, "Here comes that boring Cyril Stable-lad!"'

'Boring?' Molly asked, puzzled. 'I thought they liked you.'

29

'Oh, I knew they didn't mean it,' Cyril chuckled. 'They loved my jokes, they really did. "Here!" I'd cry. "Why did the cow jump over the moon?"

' "Because the sun wasn't out," Charles the cook would say.

' "You've heard it," I'd complain.

' "Of course I've heard it. Everyone has. You told us it last week . . . and the week before, you boring little toe-rag." '

Cyril continued, 'Nasty piece of work that Charles the cook. He was French. From France, you know. That's over the seas I think. Anyway, he talked a bit funny and I don't think he understood my jokes. At least he never laughed at them. He never laughed at much, come to that. The only time I ever saw him really laugh was when he caught me testing his pigeon soup— just testing it, mind you, not pinching a bit like he tried to make out. I swallowed too much and scalded my tongue. He laughed till the tears ran down his warty face. I didn't see the joke myself.'

'Neither would I,' Molly said gently, but she had to smother a giggle.

'And he was a snob too, that Charles the cook. Potato broth wasn't good enough for him, oh no. He had to mix garden weeds in the food—herbs, he called them—and funny bits of animals. He even used to cook *snails* for my master's dinner. Snails! Can you imagine that?'

Molly shook her head. Cyril leaned closer to the dark-haired girl and lowered his phantom voice to a whisper. 'And you'll never believe this . . .'

'Go on,' Molly urged.

'He once sent me chasing all around the castle pond looking for *frogs*! Frogs. Frogs! Yeuch! Said he was going to cut off their legs and serve them to his lordship.'

'I don't believe it,' Molly gasped in mock horror.

'I said you wouldn't,' the ghost reminded her.

Cyril fell silent till the only sound in the courtyard was the crackle of the torches. At last the girl spoke. 'Tell me about Molly,' she said. 'And the treasure-trap.'

And in a silent shadow the fat figure of Wilkin T Wilkins stirred. 'Yes,' he hissed softly. 'Tell us all about the treasure!'

'Molly!' Cyril sighed. Across his ghost-grey face there fell the faintest pink glow of a blush. And on his pinched lips a tiny smile began to flicker. 'Molly was a scullery maid. A lovely girl. Chestnut hair, green eyes and teeth that shone like butter. And she was madly in love with me!' the ghost gloated.

'Mad to love someone like you,'

Wilkin T muttered spitefully. But Cyril was too tangled in a five-hundred-year-old memory to hear him.

CHAPTER SEVEN

MOLLY THE MAID

Cyril the ghost hugged himself happily as he remembered Molly the maid. 'I could tell that she was in love with me because she always said such nasty things to me.'

'Nasty?' asked Molly, puzzled.

'That was so the others would never guess how she felt about me,' Cyril explained.

'I see,' Molly said, but in truth she found it hard to believe.

'I used to sit next to her at supper and say good-evening.

' "What do you want, you boring little toad?" she'd ask.

' "Here, Molly," I'd say. "Why did the chicken cross the road?"

' "To get to the other side," she'd say with a yawn.

' "You've heard it," I'd tease.

' "Every day for the past two years, you smelly little weasel," she'd reply.'

34

'That wasn't a very loving thing to say,' said Molly as she sat by the ghost's side.

'Oh,' Cyril chuckled cheerfully, 'but it was true. I did smell. You'd niff a bit if you slept with the horses. And Molly the maid had a very fussy nose. "If you'll excuse me I'll just go and sit at the other end of the table," she'd say. "This smell is putting me off my soup."

'"Aye," I told her. "It's the funny herbs that Charles puts in." To tell the truth the soup smelt funny to me too. And off she'd go to sit next to Charles—of course I knew she only did that to make me jealous.'

'Was she *never* nice to you?' Molly asked.

Cyril's ghostly hand scratched his phantom head. 'Only on that last day . . . the day I died.'

'Would you like to tell me about it—or would it upset you too much?' the girl asked.

Cyril shook his head. 'It happened like this. I got up at sunrise that day and mucked out the stables. Then, before I groomed his lordship's horse, I decided to slip into the kitchen for a bite of breakfast. See if there were a few scraps left from the master's feast the night before. And who do you think was there in the kitchen washing the pots?' Cyril asked.

'Molly the maid?' the girl asked eagerly.

'Exactly,' Cyril giggled. 'Molly. Alone at last. I slipped behind her quietly and slid my arm around her waist. "Guess who?" I cried and she gave me a playful swipe around the head with the frying pan she had in her hand. I think I must have passed out, because the next thing I remember was her pouring a jug of dish-water over my face. "Get up, you stupid little sparrow-brain; and don't ever sneak up on me like that again," she said. I staggered to

my feet and steadied myself against the table. "What do you want anyway, you turnip-faced clown?" she asked. Mad about me she was.

'"I've just come into the kitchen for a bite," I said. Then she did a very strange thing. She took hold of my hand. "Hello, hello!" I thought. "This is my lucky day!" and she bit it!

'"There you are," she said. "You've had a bite, now get back to work." Well, I was so overcome I asked her to marry me,' Cyril said.

'And what did she say to that?' the girl asked.

'Oh, she said yes, of course,' Cyril replied.

And even Wilkin T, hiding in the shadows, was surprised to hear it.

'She said *yes*?' Molly muttered

weakly.

'More or less . . . Her exact words were, "I'll marry you on the day you can fill this frying-pan with gold . . . which will be never, you spotty little worm."'

'So what did you do?' Molly breathed.

'Oh, I took the frying-pan from her and set off to fill it with gold from my master's treasure room,' Cyril explained.

'But you didn't get it?' Molly asked sadly.

'I *got* it all right. The trouble was I couldn't get out with it alive. The gold is still here now in this castle—and so am I.'

Molly jumped to her feet. 'And can you show me where it is?' she asked excitedly.

'I'll show you the treasure store, but you'll never beat the treasure-trap,' Cyril said. 'Even the journey is dangerous for anyone still alive. But if you want to take the risk then follow me.'

The phantom floated to his feet

and drifted over the moon-washed courtyard to a flight of steep stone steps.

Suddenly a whining voice cut across the cobblestones. 'Wait! You aren't going treasure-hunting without me!' And Wilkin T Wilkins stepped out of the shadows with a greedy grin on his froggy face.

CHAPTER EIGHT

THE CHAMBER OF TERRORS

'So, what is this treasure-trap, you boring little bucket of pig-food?' Wilkin T asked rudely.

'You'll see when we get there, sir,' Cyril the ghost said.

'And if you couldn't get out of the trap then how come you're here now? Eh? Answer that!' Wilkin T went on.

Molly was becoming cross at hearing the poor ghost spoken to like that. 'Cyril's already told you, Wilkin. He's a ghost!' she snapped.

'Hah! I don't believe in ghosts,' the fat boy sneered. 'Now, tell us the way to the treasure.'

Cyril turned and floated in front of Wilkin T. 'Since I died, the castle has changed. No one lives here any more.'

'Not surprised,' Wilkin T screeched. 'Haven't even got electric lights.'

Cyril didn't seem to hear him. He just went on, 'So now the castle is open for people to visit . . . and to make the place more popular they filled the dungeons with people made of wax. They call it *The Chamber of Terrors.* I'm afraid we'll have to go through there on our way to the treasure store.'

'Hah!' the fat boy jeered. 'Take more than a few overgrown candles to scare Wilkin T Wilkins.'

'Well, I'm a bit scared,' Molly admitted. Better dead scared than dead-dead, Mr Toon had said. Then she added kindly, 'I'm glad I've got Cyril here to look after me.'

The ghost seemed to grow and glow with pride as he led the way towards the dim stairway that led down to the dungeons. Here the flaming torches had little air to blow away the smoke. The passages were filled with a yellow-brown mist and the sooty air stung Molly's eyes. Even their footsteps fell deadly in the thick air.

Wilkin T Wilkins led the way. He didn't need Cyril's help to find the chamber. Arrows pointed the way and signs warned, *No children; Visitors with weak hearts should not pass beyond this point; Enter at your own risk;* and *You have been warned.*

Cyril said quietly, 'I often follow visitors down here and listen while Mr Toon the caretaker shows them round. I know the story behind each waxwork figure backwards.'

'What's this then, you wretched weed?' Wilkin asked as he peered into the door of the first dungeon. The figure of a huge man in ancient clothes held the figure of an old man over his head.

Molly gasped. 'Don't they look real?' And it was true. The torch-light flickered on the glassy eyes of the models and made them look alive.

'That was the second Earl of Batwing,' Cyril said, 'and the old gentleman was his Uncle Arthur; the Earl grew tired of the old man's moaning. One day he moaned that he was thirsty . . . so the Earl threw him in the moat and said, "Drink That!"'

'Good for him!' Wilkin T cackled.

'Could he swim?' Molly asked in horror.

'Not with that stone block tied to his

neck he couldn't,' Cyril said sadly. And Molly, peering more closely, saw the model had a weight tied with rough rope round it.

'Horrible man,' she shuddered.

But Wilkin T was already at the second cell and peering through the bars. 'This one's a bit boring—just some people in fancy dress having a party.'

Cyril glided alongside the frog-faced boy and said, 'That's the fourth Duchess of Batwing. She invited rich guests to the castle for supper—then she poisoned them and stole their riches. That's where the treasure of Batwing Castle came from, you know.'

Molly could see that the well-dressed wax model of a man at the table was clutching at his throat and choking on the poisoned wine. The dummy Duchess looked on and laughed. But Wilkin T was already goggling at the next model. 'This one's moving,' he said and for once his voice had a shiver in its squeak.

As Molly ran to his side she saw a shapeless form covered in a white sheet that flapped its fearsome arms at them. 'What's that, Cyril?'

Cyril shrugged. 'That's the ghost of Batwing Castle,' he sighed.

'But *you're* the ghost of Batwing Castle,' Molly said.

'I know . . . but the man who made the model never saw me,' Cyril said. 'That's what he thinks I look like.'

'But it moved!' Wilkin T said, cross that he'd been so scared.

'Something Mr Toon calls a *motor* makes it move,' Cyril said.

Wilkin T stomped off to the last cell and peered in. 'Huh! Here's another one of those stupid moving models,' he snapped. He read a notice on the door. 'The thirteenth Duke, a vampire known as the Bloodsucker of Batwing.'

'Oh, but that one's not supposed to move,' Cyril said softly.

CHAPTER NINE

THE WALKING WAXWORK

'But that waxwork *did* move, I tell you,' Wilkin T croaked. 'I am the richest boy in Toominster and I'm never wrong.'

'In that case you'd better run for your life,' Cyril said suddenly. 'Run, Molly, run!' He tried to tug her back down the corridor but his phantom fingers were too weak.

'I don't understand,' she said with a frown.

'Ohh,' Cyril moaned. 'Don't you see? There is a wax model of the ghost of Batwing Castle and there is a *real* ghost of Batwing Castle. That's me!'

'I still don't see . . .' Molly began.

'Well, there is a wax model of the vampire duke and there is a *real* vampire duke—of course he only comes to life when it's a full moon,' the ghost explained.

'But tonight's a full moon,' Molly said.

'Exactly!' Cyril groaned. 'The wax model of the vampire duke doesn't move, so that thing in the cell must be . . .'

'The real vampire?' Wilkin T finished. He gave a shaky giggle. 'But I don't believe in vampires,' he said.

'I suppose you won't believe it when he starts to suck your blood,' Cyril argued.

'I'm not scared,' Wilkin T whined. 'If this vampire is so fearsome then how come you aren't running?' he asked.

'Because I have no blood to suck,' Cyril hissed. 'Now please get out.'

'Not without the treasure,' Wilkin T said and he sounded a little more sure of himself.

'Molly, please!' the ghost begged.

Molly swallowed hard. 'Not without the treasure,' she said. 'Perhaps we could tiptoe past this vampire,' she said.

'Nothing has sharper ears than a vampire!' Cyril argued.

'And nothing is lighter on its feet than Wilkin T Wilkins in search of treasure,' the fat boy boasted. 'Watch this.'

Wilkin T lifted his right foot high into the air. Ever so slowly he stretched it forward to step past the door of the Batwing Bloodsucker. Gently, he placed his foot on the floor, more softly than a fly on a feather.

From inside the cell came a cold cackle. 'Welcome to my lair. Do come in!'

'Er, no thanks, just passing by,' Wilkin T whimpered.

The old wooden door of the cell creaked open. A black-cloaked figure stepped out. A wide-brimmed hat

shaded the top of the face but the purple mouth could be seen with its ice-white fangs.

The withered white hand reached out and grasped Wilkin T's wrist firmly and started to pull the boy towards the door. The fat boy was stiffer than the waxwork models.

Molly dashed boldly forward. 'Stop it!' she cried. 'Let him go!'

The figure in black shot out its free hand and grabbed her too. She struggled but she was dragged with Wilkin T into the gloomy dungeon.

The cell had been made to look like a vampire's den. A coffin stood in the middle of the floor. A wax figure stood with a wooden stake, ready to plunge it into the heart of the wax vampire in the coffin. As Molly gave one last desperate tug her hand came free of the man in black. The man gave a squawk, stumbled backwards and tripped over the coffin. A strange gargling sound came from his throat. Molly thought she could make out words.

'Oh, gawd,' the figure choked. 'Me

teeth . . . me fangs have come out and stuck in me throat!'

The wide black hat rolled away from the man's face. Molly found herself looking into a huge eye filled with panic.

'Mr Toon!' she cried.

'Me teeth!' he wheezed.

Molly jumped forward, pulled the old man's jaw open and pushed her fingers into the gaping mouth. A moment later she pulled a set of white plastic fangs from the caretaker's throat.

The old man lay panting and groaning on the floor. Slowly he dragged himself up and sank on to the edge of the open coffin.

Wilkin T Wilkins stepped forward and snorted, 'See, what did I tell you? There are no such things as vampires!'

'But there are, son, there are!' Mr Toon managed to pant. 'I was only trying to scare you off before the *real* Batwing Bloodsucker gets his fangs into you. Because, when he does, he'll suck you drier than an elephant's ear . . . and leave you deader than a waxwork's wig!'

CHAPTER TEN

THE BATWING BLOODSUCKER

Wilkin T Wilkins glared at Mr Toon angrily. The old man had scared him for a while and the skinny girl had seen him scared. 'I told you that the smelly little man only wanted the treasure for himself. Well, he's not going to scare me again.'

'But it's true son, there is a vampire loose in the castle tonight. Believe me,' the old man said.

'I wouldn't believe you if you told me my name was Wilkin T Wilkins,' the fat boy snarled.

'Then believe *me*,' Cyril the ghost said as he drifted through the wall into the cell.

'Hah! I believe you least of all. You go round saying you're a ghost and everyone knows there are no such things,' Wilkin T sniffed.

'But I knew the thirteenth duke when I was alive,' Cyril said.

50

'Well, that just proves that you're a liar,' the fat boy sneered. 'You say you've been dead five hundred years.'

'I have, sir,' Cyril said.

'Then the vampire would have to be five hundred years old now—and that's stupid!'

'But that's what makes him a vampire,' Cyril said. 'Vampires live for ever, so long as they get fresh blood to drink every full moon.'

'There are no such things as vampires,' the boy said. 'Now come and show me where the treasure is hidden.'

Wilkin T stalked out of the dungeon and Cyril followed with a sad shake of the head.

'Thanks for trying to help, Mr Toon,' Molly said before she joined the treasure seekers in the dim passage.

'This way,' Cyril said.

The corridor started to slope downwards into the deep heart of the castle. Green slime glistened on the wet walls and red-eyed rats squinted at them from the rafters.

Molly pulled her thin coat around her and asked, 'How did you come to

51

know the vampire, Cyril?'

'Ah, yes. You remember I told you about Charles, the French cook?' Molly nodded and Cyril went on. 'Well, one day I was haunting the castle kitchen, hoping for a glimpse of Molly the maid, when I came upon Charles reading one of his old recipe books. Suddenly he gave a great cry, "Ahh! I have it—the secret of endless life." And it seems the secret was to drink fresh blood when the moon was full.'

'But where did he get the blood from?' Molly asked with a shudder.

'At first he killed the castle cats.'

'Poor moggies,' Molly murmured.

'And then he started on the servants.'

'Not Molly the maid!' the girl gasped.

'No, no,' Cyril said with a sad smile. 'She choked on a chicken bone one evening. I remember her ghost flew past me on its way to the afterlife. "Hello, Molly," I called to her.

' "Oh, no, not you again," she said.

'I tried to cheer her up. "Heh, Molly," I said, "Why did the chicken cross the road?"

' "Look here, you boring little drip of sheepdip," she said, "If you'd just died like I've just died, then the last thing you'd want to talk about is rotten chickens!" Perhaps she was right,' the ghost groaned.

'So Charles the cook killed the servants?' Molly asked.

'Yes. One each month when the moon was full. And after all the servants had gone he killed my old master and made himself the thirteenth duke. Now he sleeps in his coffin and only rises each full moon to drink his fill of blood.'

'Do we have to pass near his coffin?' Molly said, and her mouth was dry.

'We have to,' Cyril nodded. 'But don't worry. One of his powers is to change himself into a bat and fly the world looking for his victims. Perhaps he won't be home when we get there.'

'Is it far now?' the girl asked.

'Through this archway and we're there,' the ghost replied.

Wilkin T Wilkins pushed his way past Molly and smiled his thin-lipped smile. 'You're wasting your time, you know. The treasure will be mine.'

And he stepped into the room that was cool as a tomb. A white face looked up from the oak coffin in the centre of the room.

'Good evening,' said a smooth voice with a slight French accent. 'And who are you?'

'I'm Wilkin T Wilkins, the richest boy in Toominster—as you know fine well, Mr Toon.'

'But my name is not Toon,' the figure in the coffin crooned. 'I am Charles, thirteenth Duke of Batwing Castle—have you any frogs' legs?'

CHAPTER ELEVEN

SNAKES' LEGS SNACKS

'If I had frogs' legs I'd hop out of here and away from you,' Wilkin T joked. 'You are a boring little caretaker.'

'Oh, so I'm a caretaker, am I? the Batwing Bloodsucker said softly. 'Come over here and I'll take care of you once and for all.'

Molly screamed and shrank into a corner. Wilkin T smirked at her fear.

'You don't scare me, Pop Toon,' the boy said and he walked over to the figure in the coffin.

The vampire duke sat up. Wilkin T prodded him back down with a flabby finger. 'Give up now, old man,' he said. 'You won't get the treasure. I will.'

The man in the coffin sat up again and a snarl curled his lips back to show shining yellow fangs.

'Your false teeth need a clean,' Wilkin giggled. 'Make sure you don't choke on them this time.'

'You are the one who will be choking soon,' the man growled as he rose to his feet. The vampire's head brushed the low ceiling.

Wilkin looked up at the fierce figure. 'You've grown a lot, Mr Toon,' the boy said.

The vampire stretched out a clawed hand and grasped the fat boy by the collar. 'I'm thirsty,' he hissed.

'Your nails need cutting too,' Wilkin T complained.

With one powerful hand the vampire raised the boy from the stone floor till his feet dangled in the dank air. 'Geg off. You'a 'urting nee,' Wilkin T struggled to say.

Charles, thirteenth Duke of Batwing, licked his purple lips with a rough red tongue and looked hungrily at the fat neck of Wilkin T Wilkins.

'I do not believe in vampires!' the boy said faintly and Molly didn't wait to hear more. She scrambled to the door and fled along the passage. A door stood open on her right and she pushed her way into it. Molly slammed the door and stood with her back against it, panting.

'Poor Wilkin,' she groaned. 'No one to save him. Mr Toon's too old and Cyril's too weak. No one to save him. Except me, of course,' said Molly, standing up straight. 'Molly Stone,' she said angrily, 'you are nothing but a coward. Get back into that room and save poor Wilkin.' The girl took a deep breath and hurried back along the corridor to the vampire's den.

Wilkin T Wilkins stood in the middle of the doorway and smirked. 'I told you there were no such things as vampires,' he said, then marched past her down the corridor.

'But what happened, Wilkin?' she asked.

'A vampire's no match for Wilkin T Wilkins,' he grinned as he disappeared round the corner.

Molly looked into the room, and the red eyes of the vampire gleamed back at her. He stepped towards her with a growl.

Suddenly Cyril flew between the vampire and the girl. 'No, Charles, not Molly!'

'I'm still thirsty,' the monster grumbled.

'I'll get you blood,' Cyril promised in panic. 'The sort you really like . . . frog's-leg blood and snail's blood . . . anything, only leave the girl!'

'All right, you boring little stable-boy,' the vampire said. 'If you can really get me some nice fresh frogs' legs. I haven't tasted those for a hundred and fifty years or more.'

'Oh, yes, frogs' legs, toads' legs, ants' legs, snakes' legs . . . anything!'

'Snakes don't have legs,' Charles

hissed.

'That's only because all the French cooks have cut them off to make their stews,' Cyril said. 'But I'm sure I could find some for you, sir.'

Charles licked his purple lips. 'Snakes' legs. A snack of snakes' legs. That sounds delicious. Yes. Bring me a dozen before the next full moon and I'll free the girl.'

'I agree,' the ghost said, then turned to the girl. 'Let's go quickly.'

'Wait!' the vampire snapped. 'Keep the girl somewhere safe till you return with the snakes' legs. We don't want her to escape, do we?'

'No, sir,' Cyril said with a shake of his head. 'Er, where should I keep her?'

The Batwing Bloodsucker gave a cruel chuckle. 'Somewhere where she'll stay fresh—how about the treasure-room. She'll never escape from there; after all, you didn't, you spotty little spook, did you?'

'No, sir,' Cyril mumbled miserably. 'Come along, Molly.'

'Where are we going?' the girl asked.

'To the treasure-room,' Cyril said. 'And the treasure-trap.'

To the treasure-room,' Cyril said. 'And the treasure-trap.'

CHAPTER TWELVE

THE TREASURE-TRAP

Cyril led the way through a maze of tunnels. The further they went, the smaller the tunnels became. Suddenly Cyril stopped.

'What's wrong?' Molly whispered.

'I think we're being followed,' the ghost said with a tremble in his voice.

Molly tried to look along the tunnel but the smoke from the torches made the air too thick to see. She closed her eyes tightly and tried to listen. She heard the hiss of a burning torch and the scutter of a rat. She opened her eyes again and shrugged. 'Nothing!' she said to Cyril.

Cyril shook his head. 'I was so *sure*,' he said.

'Let's hurry,' Molly said. 'Which way now?'

'Right, I think,' the ghost said.

'You're not sure?' the girl asked with a frown.

'It could be left, of course . . . or straight ahead.'

'Don't you know, Cyril?' Molly cried.

'Ah, well,' Cyril muttered. 'We've entered the part of the castle that only appears every ten years. I don't get in here too often.'

'But it will disappear at sunrise, won't it?' Molly asked.

Cyril nodded.

'And what happens if we're still here when it disappears? Do we disappear with it?' she went on.

'I think so,' Cyril said slowly.

'And what if I can't find my way out again?' Molly cried.

'It would help if I had a map,' Cyril said.

'I don't have one,' Molly moaned.

'Or a guidebook.'

'I don't have . . .' the girl began, and then stopped. She pushed a hand into her anorak pocket and pulled out a crumpled little booklet. 'Of course! Mr Toon's guidebook! I wonder if it has a plan of the old castle in it?'

Eagerly she turned the pages until she found the plan she was looking for.

'Here it is Cyril!' she cried. 'I've found it.' Molly traced a path with her finger along the passages they'd come along. 'We must be here now . . . and the treasure-room is . . .'

Before she could find it she felt a rush of cold air along the corridor. There was a glimpse of a fat, freckled face before the map was snatched from her hand and the cackling boy carried it down the corridor. 'I told you I'd get the treasure first,' he cried before he vanished into the smoky tunnel.

Molly didn't often lose her temper, but when she did she became wild as a tail-pulled tiger. 'Come back here, you frog-faced thief!' she screamed and gave chase.

'Sticks and stones may break my bones,' Wilkin's voice echoed ahead of her, 'but names can never hurt me—you patch-kneed penniless pin-brain.'

Molly rushed down the passageway after him and found herself at a corridor cross-roads. 'I went back to save you from the vampire,' she called. 'The least you could do is share the treasure with me.'

64

'More fool you,' came the jeering voice from the corridor to her left. She set off down it as fast as she could run.

But soon she reached another crossroads. 'Wilkin? Where are you?'

This time the boy was too crafty to answer. Molly felt the treasure slipping from her and tears blurred her eyes. Suddenly there was a POP in the smoky air and Cyril appeared in front of her. 'This way, Molly!' he cried, pointing to the passage on her left. The girl wiped the tears from her eyes and tumbled into the turning.

And so the chase went on. Every time Molly reached a fork in the passage Cyril was there to point the way. 'Left, Molly, left . . . you're catching him now—he's got to stop to read the map. Now right . . . and . . . carefully, Molly! Stop! Stop! STOP!'

For Molly had reached the end of the chase. Ahead of her stood an open archway. Beyond it, glimmering and glinting in the light of a hundred candles, stood a heap of gold and a rainbow of jewels. A heap as high as the roof of the room. And rolling in the middle of the heap was the happy form of the richest boy in Toominster . . . now, maybe, the world. Molly stepped forward. 'Wilkin T Wilkins you are the most selfish, unpleasant and greedy boy there ever was.'

'I know, I know,' the fat boy cackled and he rolled some more in the treasure. 'What are you going to do about it, skinny?'

'I'll show you what . . .' Molly said as she stepped through the arch.

'No, Molly, no!' Cyril screamed. But too late. Molly Stone had entered the treasure-trap.

CHAPTER THIRTEEN

THE GHOSTS OF BATWING CASTLE

Molly turned around as Cyril cried. The ghost slipped through the wall behind her. He seemed a limp and shrunken creature, more pitiful than ever. 'Oh, Molly, Molly, Molly . . . I tried to warn you!'

'Warn me? Warn me about what?' she asked. The anger she felt for Wilkin T Wilkins had faded as suddenly as it had risen. Something was wrong. She knew it. Something was out of place. It wasn't just the misery of her friend, the ghost, that warned her. There was something else.

'Now you'll die in the treasure-trap like I did,' Cyril said sadly. 'At least I'll have company.'

'What is this treasure-trap?' she asked.

'It's a one-way door,' Cyril began. He didn't need to finish. Molly understood

67

now what was wrong. She was in a room filled with treasure. But it was the only room like it in the world. It was a room without a door.

She remembered stepping through the archway. Cyril had called and she had turned round, to see the ghost slip *through* the wall. For the doorway had gone. Vanished.

The treasure store had eight walls. Each one was as solid as the other. Slowly she walked towards the wall that she thought she'd come through. It was as cold and clammy as any dungeon wall. She pushed it. She searched down the cracks between the stones and scrabbled at it till her fingernails tore.

At last she beat it with her fist.

And nothing happened.

Slowly she turned back to Wilkin T Wilkins who lay on his fat stomach and wallowed in rubies and emeralds and diamonds. 'Wilkin, we're trapped. All that money's no good at all. We can't get out!'

'Why should I want to get out? It's lovely here!' he chuckled and gurgled

like a baby in a bubblebath.

'We have to eat, Wilkin.'

'I'm not hungry.'

'We have to get home!'

'I told you, I'm running away from home—never going back now. My parents hate me anyway,' Wilkin crooned calmly.

'Wilkin, you'll die in here!'

'No I won't,' the boy said with a silly smile on his face.

'That was a one-way door, Wilkin,' Molly argued desperately.

'There is no such thing as a one-way door,' he scoffed.

'Then try walking through there!' Molly cried. The boy looked up crossly. 'Oh, all right, if you'll promise to stop nagging.'

Wilkin T rolled off the heap of treasure and strolled over to the door-wall. Without stopping he walked into the wall . . . and through it. A few moments later he popped back through. 'See. Nothing to it. Like I told you. There is no such thing as a one-way door. No such thing as ghosts. No such thing as vampires.'

Molly rushed at the spot where he had entered. She kicked, punched and butted the stones till every bone in her body ached and she ended a battered, sobbing heap on the floor. 'Oh, Cyril,' she sniffled. 'How did he do that?'

The ghost floated down gently beside her. 'Because he's a ghost, Molly, he's a ghost.'

'Since when?' the girl gasped.

'Since the vampire of Batwing Castle killed him,' Cyril said softly.

'Does Wilkin *know* he's a ghost?' Molly asked.

'I did try to tell him . . . but

he doesn't believe in ghosts—or vampires—so he didn't believe me,' Cyril said.

Molly ran a hand through her long hair. 'So, I'm the only living person in this room?' she said and the ghost nodded. 'And I'll never leave it alive,' she whispered.

Cyril stared at the blank wall and stayed silent.

'I don't want to die here,' Molly added. 'Mum and Dad would never know what happened to me.'

'They say the afterlife isn't too bad,' Cyril said warmly. It was kindly meant but the wrong thing to say.

'If it's so good then why haven't you gone there?' Molly cried, and tears began to flood her eyes.

'I'd like to . . . but I made it my job to stay and warn people about the trap.' Cyril gave a huge sigh. 'I didn't do a very good job, did I? I'm sorry, Molly. Really sorry.'

She sniffed and tried to smile. 'Never mind, Cyril. I should have listened to you at the start.'

But Cyril's thoughts were far away.

71

'I've an idea that might help you escape the treasure-trap,' he said.

CHAPTER FOURTEEN

WILKIN T'S TREASURE

Cyril slipped out through the wall and left Molly alone with the ghost of Wilkin T Wilkins. Her eyelids felt heavy. 'Do you have a watch, Wilkin?' she asked.

'Of course I do. A two-thousand pound, solid gold thirty-five jewel watch. It gives the date, the day of the week, tells you the temperature and gives you a weather forecast,' he said smugly.

'But does it tell you the time?' Molly asked.

'I think so,' Wilkin T muttered and pressed several buttons. 'It's . . . er . . . eleven o'clock.'

'It was midnight when we entered the castle hours ago,' Molly argued.

'I know that!' Wilkin said peering at the dial. 'It's eleven in New York stupid . . . so it must be about four o'clock in the morning in Batwing.'

'Four o'clock!' Molly said. 'Sunrise soon . . . if Cyril doesn't get back in time I'll disappear with the castle, or be stuck here for ever.'

'Lovely,' Wilkin T sighed. 'Just think . . . here *for ever* . . . heaven!'

Molly thought for a while. 'Wilkin,' she said.

'Mmm?' the boy answered, carelessly running his fingers through a heap of golden coins.

'If you really want to stay here for ever you could take Cyril's job.'

The fat boy sat up sharply. 'Do you think he'd let me?'

'I'm sure he would,' Molly said carefully.

'What work would I have to do?' Wilkin T asked, his eyes narrowing to cunning black slits.

'Guard the treasure . . . warn people about the treasure-trap.'

'There's no such thing. That's just a story to scare people away.'

'Perhaps it is . . . but you could be the one to tell that story,' Molly pointed out.

'I could,' Wilkin T agreed. 'Then I'd

be able to keep the treasure all for myself.'

'You would,' Molly said.

'And what would skinny Cyril get out of it?' the fat ghost asked.

'He'd be free to leave the castle and go in search of his Molly,' the girl said.

'If he's daft enough to want that rather than the treasure, then let him,' Wilkin T declared.

At that moment Cyril slipped through the wall. His eyes flickered excitedly as he spoke. 'Ready, Molly?' he said. 'The door will open for just a moment. You have to run out when you see the gap in the wall.'

'But how . . .' Molly began.

'Don't ask now. I'll tell you later . . . ready?'

The girl stood by the wall and stared at the solid stone. Suddenly she saw it flicker and fade. She closed her eyes and rushed forward. She waited for the crunch of stone but instead she shot through into the smoky air of the corridor and bumped into Mr Toon the caretaker.

The old man tumbled to the ground

and Molly bent to help him up. 'Oh, Mr Toon,' she said, frowning. 'You look ill. Did I hurt you?'

'No . . . just weak,' he gasped. 'Vampire . . . had to give him a litre of me blood to get past.'

'But how did you open the door for me?' Molly asked.

'Don't talk now,' Cyril moaned. 'It's sunrise soon. The tunnels will vanish with the ghost part of the castle. You have to be out of here by then or you'll never escape alive.'

Molly grabbed the arm of the old caretaker and half-carried, half-dragged him through the maze as Cyril led the way and urged them on with cries of 'Hurry, Molly, hurry.'

At last they reached the entrance to the Batwing Bloodsucker's cave and Cyril said, 'You can rest now, Molly. We're in the safe part of the castle.'

The girl sank to the ground next to the panting caretaker. 'Thanks, Cyril,' she said. 'But how did you do it?'

'I knew the door must open for a moment every time a living person passed through it,' Cyril explained. 'I thought that if I could get a living person to step *half-way* through it then you should be able to slip out as the door opened to let him in.'

'And it worked. Oh, Cyril, you're the cleverest ghost in the world,' she said.

'No he's not,' came a nasty voice from the doorway. Charles, the Batwing Bloodsucker glared at them with fire-red eyes. 'He forgot that he promised to keep you there for me! He may have got you out of the treasure-trap . . . but he'll never get you past me—alive!'

CHAPTER FIFTEEN

THE GHOST CASTLE

'You lied to me, Cyril. You said you'd keep her fresh till the next full moon. Now you're trying to help her to escape!' the vampire snarled. The tall monster stepped closer to Molly. She jumped to her feet and clutched her hands to her throat.

There was a 'POP!' and Cyril appeared in front of the Batwing Bloodsucker. 'Tell me, Charles, why did the cow jump over the moon?'

'Get out of my way you boring little stable-boy,' the vampire grunted.

'Bet you can't tell me, can you? Can you?' Cyril gabbled.

'What are you talking about?'

'It's a riddle—if you can answer it I'll . . . I'll let you have the blood of the caretaker too!' Cyril promised.

'Thanks very much, son,' the old man moaned. His face was as grey as the whiskers on his chin and he'd hardly the strength to sit up on the cold stone floor.

The vampire took his eyes off the girl and started to pick at his yellow fangs with his long brown fingernails. 'What was the question again?' he said.

'Why did the cow jump over the moon?' Cyril said.

The vampire started to pace up and down the corridor muttering to himself. 'Why did the cow jump over the moon?'

Cyril began to tremble. His eyes flickered and he kept glancing at the castle walls.

The vampire stalked back to where the ghost stood. 'I've heard this one before,' he said in his harsh voice.

'That's right,' Cyril said. 'I asked you this about five hundred years ago when you were the castle cook and I was the stable-lad.'

'Five hundred years is a long time to remember something,' Charles the vampire complained. His red eyes half closed as he thought. 'Why did the cow jump over the moon?' he muttered and walked away again to think.

Cyril glanced at the castle walls again and he whispered to Molly, 'Just another minute—if we can keep him away from you for just another minute you'll be safe!'

Molly nodded though she didn't understand. She began to count. 'Fifty seconds now,' she thought.

The vampire came back to where she stood. 'Why did the cow jump over the moon? I remember the answer now!' the vampire gloated.

Forty seconds. Just forty seconds.

'The cow jumped over the moon . . .

to get to the other side!' the monster crowed, and he reached out a clawed hand for the girl.

'Wrong!' Cyril cried.

And thirty seconds still remained.

'Eh?' the vampire hissed.

'Wrong!' Cyril said. 'That's why the chicken crossed the road—but it's not why the cow jumped over the moon.'

Just twenty seconds to go.

'It's why *my* cow jumped over the moon,' the monster bellowed. 'Now let me take the girl.' Again he reached towards Molly.

'If you do that you'll never know the real answer,' Cyril said.

And ten seconds were left.

'Oh, very well, tell me, why *did* the cow jump over the moon?'

Cyril giggled. 'Because the sun wasn't out.'

'Because the sun wasn't out!' the vampire muttered. 'I don't get it.'

'You will in three seconds,' Cyril promised, 'because by then the sun will be out. And vampires can't live in the light of the sun.'

'There's no sun down here anyway

you porridge-brained pipsqueak,' the Batwing Bloodsucker pointed out.

'No,' Cyril agreed, 'but at sunrise the ghost castle fades. See. That wall is growing faint already.'

As Molly watched she could see the sky growing brighter, shining through the wall. A blood-red ray of sunlight broke through the pearl grey cloud and struck the vampire. For a moment he stood as frozen as his waxwork model, then he turned to a powder as fine as moon-dust. The morning breeze broke through the last of the ghost-wall and scattered the powder to the corners of the world.

'Oh, thank you, Cyril,' Molly said . . . but Cyril was gone too. Vanished like the ghost-castle he'd lived in. 'You're free now, Cyril,' she said to the empty air. 'Hope you find your Molly!'

CHAPTER SIXTEEN

SUNRISE OVER BATWING

The caretaker struggled to his feet, dusted down his old blue uniform and yawned. He looked around the sad and shabby ruin that was Batwing Castle and his golf-ball eye blinked at a girl in patched and faded jeans. He looked like a man who'd just woken from a strange dream. He walked over to where the girl stood talking to the thin, cold air. 'Caught me asleep at my post, miss,' he said. She just smiled and gazed around the ruins. He went on, 'It's funny, but sometimes I dream that this old castle is larger and grander.'

'Perhaps it is,' Molly said quietly, her soft black hair rising like a bat's wing in the fresh morning wind. 'Perhaps the old castle returns when the moon is full on Friday the thirteenth.'

'Ah, you've heard that tale, have you?' the old man chuckled.

'You don't believe it?' Molly asked.

84

The caretaker sighed. 'Last night, when the moon magic was strongest, I think I had a funny dream!'

'Only a dream?'

'Only a dream . . . or maybe I was awake and perhaps it was the ghost of the old castle that I saw,' he joked.

'There are no such things as ghosts, a boy once told me,' Molly murmured.

Mr Toon scratched his grey-bristled chin, and rubbed a sore spot on his throat. 'Funny, I think I once knew a boy who said the same thing.'

'I think you did,' Molly said.

'He was a strange boy,' the old man said. 'He said he was rich and yet he wanted more—said he was the richest boy in Toominster, yet he was too mean to buy one of my guidebooks.'

'Wilkin!' Molly gasped. 'It wasn't a dream, then! He was here last night!'

'Last night!' said the caretaker laughing. 'Bless you, no! He was here twelve years ago or more. Last time the full moon fell on Friday the thirteenth.'

'Not twelve years! He was here last night,' Molly argued. 'I came in his car. A red sports car!' But when she looked through the castle gate the road was empty; not even a tyre-track to show a car had ever been there.

'No, twelve years ago,' Mr Toon insisted. 'I remember the fuss they made when he disappeared. I told him he should have bought a guidebook. They found his car but they never found him.'

Molly shook her head in wonder. 'I was sure I met him last night.'

'Perhaps he's just another ghost,' the caretaker said with a chuckle. 'Or perhaps I'm getting old.' He looked at the girl as if seeing her for the first time. 'You're out and about early, aren't you? It's barely sunrise.'

'I've been out treasure hunting,' Molly explained.

'Oh, that old game,' the old man laughed. 'That old story about the treasure!'

'You don't believe it, then?' Molly asked.

'They come, they search, but they always go away empty handed. Still, they seem to enjoy themselves. Always have exciting tales to tell of meeting vampires,' Mr Toon snorted with a shake of his head.

'You don't believe in vampires either?' Molly asked.

'No ghosts, no vampires,' and he rubbed his sore throat again.

'And no treasure,' the girl went on, hugging her thin anorak to her body.

'So, miss, you didn't get your treasure?' the caretaker asked.

'No,' she said. 'A boy beat me to it. But if being rich means being like him I'm better off without it. Goodbye, Mr Toon.'

'Goodbye, Molly,' he said . . . and suddenly he wondered how he came to know her name. And surely he hadn't told her *his* name!

The caretaker of Batwing Castle watched the girl thoughtfully as she set off down the winding road for home.

The sun rose on the tumble of stones that used to be a castle. And, deep beneath the ruin, the ghosts went back to sleep.